THE DRAGONS WITHOUT EYES

And Other Chinese Folktales

25 Stories to Hear, Read, Tell, and Discuss

Phebe Xu Gray, PhD

T0149087

Pro Lingua Associates

Pro Lingua Associates, Publishers
P.O. Box 1348
Brattleboro, Vermont 05302 USA
Office: 802-257-7779
Orders: 800-366-4775
Email: info@ProLinguaAssociates.com
WebStore www.ProLinguaAssociates.com
SAN: 216-0579

*At Pro Lingua
our objective is to foster an approach
to learning and teaching that we call
interplay, the interaction of language
learners and teachers with their materials,
with the language and culture,
and with each other in active, creative
and productive play.*

ISBN: 978-0-86647-278-4

Thanks to Cai Xi Silver for her calligraphy.

This book was designed and set by Cape Cod Compositors, Inc., in Pembroke, Massachusetts, and printed and bound by Edwards Brothers, Inc., in Ann Arbor, Michigan.

Illustrations by Kay Kopper.

The photograph of the Chinese temple dragon used on page 81 by Christine Gonsalves, Dreamstime.com Agency.

Printed in the United States of America.

First edition 2008. 1500 copies in print.

Contents

The basic idea of this collection of tales is quite simple. People like to read, tell, listen to, and talk about stories. In this collection there are **25 famous folktales** from China, reflecting the long history and ancient culture of this important country. Each tale is presented as a reading passage on one page, and on the backside of the page, there is a list of **prompts** for telling the story. The stories progress from short (about 100 words) and easy, to longer (200 words) and more difficult.

In addition to the tales, the book contains a section of **dictations** (Part 2) for each of the stories. Following the dictations section there are three pages of **discussion prompts** (Part 3). Finally, there are short passages that provide **background** (Part 4) to the time and place of the story, with notes about the culture.

A **Story CD** is available for use as an optional listening comprehension activity and pronunciation model. The dictations are also available as a separate set of **Dictation CDs**. Also available is a **Teacher's Handbook** with photocopyable vocabulary exercises and verb cards. The Handbook is available as a separate booklet, or for free downloading from the Pro Lingua website. A **Chinese Version of the Stories** in ideographic characters and Pinyin is also available as a booklet or for downloading.

The book is designed for **English language learners**. However, **Chinese language learners**, as well as **Chinese heritage speakers** will benefit from these stories, especially since they provide background about Chinese culture. The book can also serve as a resource book for the teacher of mainstream students who are studying China. Elementary and kindergarten school teachers will find the book a useful source for telling Chinese folktales.

The book can be used in a variety of ways. Obviously, the tales can be used as readings for language development, and/or simply for entertainment. The pages in this book are detachable. This allows the users to remove the pages and use them for story cards for the purpose of developing oral and aural language skills through storytelling. The background information can be used to enhance the user's understanding of the history and culture of the world's largest population. The discussion prompts and dictations can be used to improve the user's linguistic skills. The following is a suggested procedure for maximizing the material, although the parts of the book may be used in a variety of ways.

1. **Tell the story** to the learners (books closed). The learners listen. One variation is to first play the CD. Although the CD is an optional component, the voices on the CD provide the listeners with an alternative to hearing only your voice.

2. **Check for general comprehension.** You can simply ask specific questions or ask the learners to tell you what they understood.

3. **Have the learners read** the story silently and individually. Tell them to note any words they are not sure of.

4. **Check again for comprehension and vocabulary gaps** by leading the learners toward a reasonably accurate comprehension of the story. While doing this, elicit vocabulary problems and help the learners' search for meanings.

5. **Dictate the story** using the dictations in Part 2. The lines have been broken into phrases. First read the entire sentence. Then read it phrase by phrase, allowing time for the learners to write each phrase. Finally, read the entire sentence again.

6. **Ask the WH questions** following the dictations. This activity can help consolidate the meaning of the story and also provide practice in differentiating WH questions and responding appropriately to them.

7. **The learners use the prompts to tell the story** from memory. This can work well as a pair activity as the partners take turns telling the story to each other. One partner looks at the prompts and attempts to relate the story while the other looks at the story and helps. They can then swap partners and tell and listen again with a different person. After a few minutes you can ask for a volunteer to stand and tell the story from memory.

8. **Discuss the stories** in small groups or as a class using the prompts in Part 3. Some of the stories are "entertainment" stories, and some are "instructional" stories that impart a lesson. There are two questions for each story. In general, the first question involves comprehension of the story line, and the second one is about the lesson (moral). The lesson is not overtly stated in the story in order to stimulate discussion among the learners about the lesson of the story. Not all stories have obvious lessons.

9. Finally, and optionally, have the learners **read the story backgrounds** in Part 4. Less proficient learners may have difficulty with these readings. In that case, you can summarize the key points to them. Many of these background readings can be used as a springboard to further research on China. For example, in Story 1, "The Snake with Feet," the Chinese zodiac is mentioned. A quick exploration of the Internet could be conducted to learn more about the zodiac and the Chinese calendar.

As mentioned earlier, the book may be used in a variety of ways. Some possibilities:

1. **Trading Stories.** Give each student a different story—easier stories for the less proficient. Circulate and help the learners understand their stories. When learners feel they can tell the story using only the prompts, or from memory, they stand up and look for another person who is standing. They tell each other their stories. Then they take another look at the story, split up and find another person to tell. They may do this three or four times, each time becoming more proficient.

2. **Story-A-Day.** Each day one student tells a story to the class.

3. **Write with Prompts.** Have the learners look at the prompts page of a story they are familiar with and write the story.

4. **Listen and Write.** Read a story to the learners, preferably one that has already been studied. They write it out from memory. They can compare with a friend, listen again, or hand it in.

5. **Act It Out.** Give a story to a group of students (The number depends on the story) and have them perform it for their classmates. It may be necessary to have a narrator as well as actors.

6. **Direct/Indirect Speech Practice.** Have the students rewrite the direct quotes as indirect, and vice versa.

7. **Develop a content-based unit** on China using other sources. Use the collection as a complement to the unit. Engaging the learners actively in reading, telling, writing, even acting out a story, can help make a social studies unit come alive.

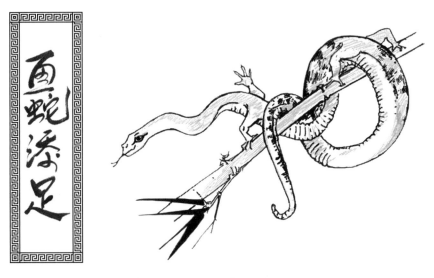

The Snake with Feet

O ne day, a rich man in the region of Chu gave his servants a bottle of wine. He told them to share it. There were many servants, but not much wine. The servants decided to play a game. They decided to draw snakes. The first one to finish the drawing would win. He would drink the wine by himself.

Servant Wang finished his drawing first. However, he decided to add feet to his snake. While Servant Wang was adding feet to his snake, Servant Li finished his drawing. Servant Wang did not drink the wine.

1

The Snake
with Feet

rich man
servants
wine
share
many
game
draw snakes
Wang
finished
added
Servant Li

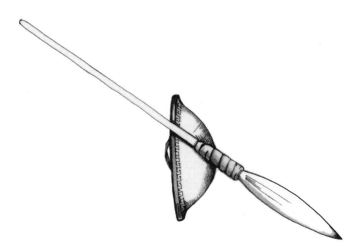

The Spear and the Shield

In ancient times, different regions of China fought each other. Once, a weapons seller tried to sell his weapons in the market place. He held his spear high in the air. "These are the sharpest spears in the world!" he said. "They can penetrate the strongest shields!"

Then the man held his shield high in the air. He boasted, "These are the strongest shields in the world. They will stop the sharpest spears!"

A listener in the crowd shouted to him, "Sir, what would happen if your spears attacked your shields?" The merchant was speechless. He did not know what to say.

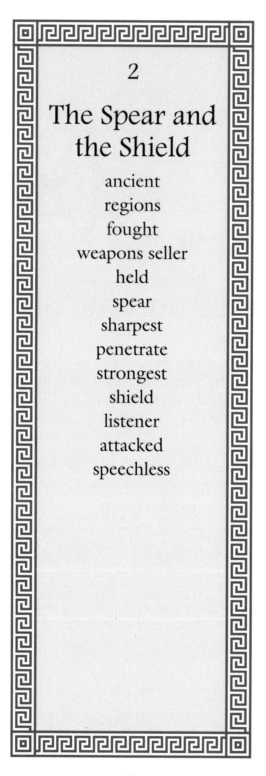

2

The Spear and the Shield

ancient
regions
fought
weapons seller
held
spear
sharpest
penetrate
strongest
shield
listener
attacked
speechless

The Pearl and Its Case

A merchant had a valuable pearl. He tried to sell it for a high price. He was not successful. No one wanted to spend a lot of money for the pearl.

He decided to make a beautiful case for the pearl. He used expensive wood. He decorated the case with pretty stones. He put the pearl inside and displayed it in its case.

A buyer came by. The display looked beautiful. He was attracted to it and bought the pearl and its case. After he bought the display, he gave the pearl back to the merchant and walked away with the case.

3

The Pearl and Its Case

merchant
valuable
pearl
high price
spend
case
expensive wood
decorated
pretty stones
displayed
buyer
looked
attracted
bought
gave back
walked away

Playing Music to a Cow

A famous musician was known for his great skill in playing the Chinese zither. Everyone loved his music. However, sometimes his behavior seemed silly.

One day, he was traveling in the countryside. He saw a cow eating grass in a pasture. The scene inspired him. He started to play the zither in front of the cow, enjoying the beauty of his own music. The cow, on the other hand, was not interested in his music. It kept on eating and behaving like a cow.

The musician did not understand why the cow did not appreciate his music.

4

Playing Music
to a Cow

famous musician
skill
Chinese zither
behavior
silly
countryside
cow
pasture
scene
inspired
enjoying
not interested
kept on
appreciate

The Dragons without Eyes

Zhang was a famous artist in the Nanbei Dynasty. The emperor liked his paintings very much. He asked Zhang to paint four dragons for the Buddhist Temple in the capital.

Zhang finished the painting in three days. The dragons looked very real. However, there were no eyes on the dragons. Zhang said, "If I paint eyes on the dragons, they will fly away."

Nobody believed him. Zhang told them to come and watch. He finished painting eyes on two of the dragons. Suddenly, clouds gathered and thunder roared in the sky. The two dragons with eyes came to life and flew away!

5

The Dragons without Eyes

famous artist
Nanbei Dynasty
emperor
paintings
four dragons
Buddhist Temple
three days
real
no eyes
fly away
believed
watch
clouds gathered
thunder roared
came to life

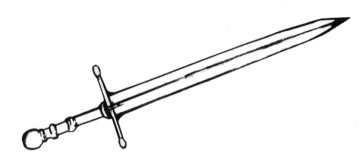

The Lost Sword

Once upon a time, a man was crossing the Yangtze River in a boat. The Yangtze is famous for the beautiful scenery along its banks. The man stood by the edge of the boat to enjoy the scenery. Unfortunately his sword accidentally fell into the water. He immediately marked a spot on the boat to show where the sword fell.

His fellow traveler urged him to jump into the water to get the sword. The man said, "Look at this mark. This is where my sword fell. When the boat reaches the shore, I will jump in the water at this marked spot to find the sword."

6

The Lost Sword

crossing

Yangtze River

scenery

banks

edge

unfortunately

sword

accidentally

immediately

marked

fellow traveler

urged

reaches

shore

find

The Money Sign

People used gold and silver coins as money in ancient China. However, they did not generally deposit their money in a bank as we do nowadays.

Once, a man inherited three hundred pieces of silver from his father. The man was afraid someone might steal the silver, so he decided to hide the coins. He decided to bury them in his back yard. However, he was still afraid it was not safe enough, so he put up a sign. It said, "There is no money hidden in this spot."

A neighbor, Little Er, saw the sign and stole the money at night. Little Er put up another sign. It said, "Little Er did not steal the money that was hidden here."

7

The Money Sign

gold and silver coins
deposit
bank
inherited
pieces
afraid
steal
hide
bury
back yard
safe enough
sign
hidden
neighbor
stole
another sign

Monkey Math

Once there was a man who loved monkeys. He kept many monkeys at home as pets. However, it was very expensive to keep the monkeys because they required lots of bananas and other fresh fruit.

One day he made a proposal to them. He said, "Dear friends, I am getting poor now. I can only give you three bananas in the morning, and four bananas at night."

The monkeys protested. They said, "No! We need more bananas! We like bananas!"

The man pretended to think very hard. Then he said, "Ok, I will sacrifice. How about four bananas in the morning and three at night?" The monkeys thought it was a good deal. They gladly accepted the second proposal.

This is what we call monkey math.

8

Monkey Math

monkeys
pets
expensive
required
bananas and fruit
proposal
poor
only
protested
pretended
sacrifice
how about
good deal
accepted

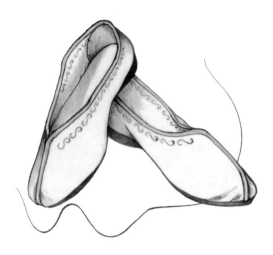

The Man Buying Shoes

One day in the ancient state of Zheng, a man named Zheng wanted to buy a pair of shoes in the market. Before he went, he measured his feet with a string, and left for the market.

After traveling for twenty miles, he arrived at the shoe shop in the market. It took him a long time to select the style. Finally, he reached for the string to determine the shoe size. Then he realized he had left the string at home. Leaving the shoes behind, he returned home to get the string. However, by the time he came back to the market with the string, the shop was closed.

People asked him why he did not try on the shoes. Zheng said, "I know the measurement of the string, but I don't know the measurement of my own feet."

9

The Man
Buying Shoes

ancient
Zheng
a pair of shoes
measured
string
arrived
select
to determine
size
realized
at home
to get
came back
closed
try on
measurement

The Fox and the Tiger

One day, the king of the forest, tiger, caught a fox. He was pleased because now he would have a good meal.

The fox, however, was very clever. He told the tiger, "The Heavens sent me to be the King of the Forest. If you eat me, God will punish you." The tiger was very doubtful that the fox was the King of the Forest. The fox tried to convince him. He said, "Let's take a walk together. Please follow me. You will see how terrified other animals will be when they see me."

The fox and the tiger walked into the forest. All the animals, including the bears, fled immediately when they saw the tiger.

The fox tricked the tiger and saved his own life; the tiger, on the other hand, lost a good meal.

10

The Fox
and the Tiger

king of the forest
tiger
caught
fox
meal
clever
Heavens
eat
punish
doubtful
convince
terrified
bears
fled
tricked
saved
lost

The Promise of the Plums

General Cao was a famous military leader. Once, he led his soldiers on a long march. It was late summer and very hot. The soldiers became thirsty and tired.

It was a very difficult march, and they had to reach their destination by a certain time. The guide told him that the river where the men could drink and rest was still far away. Then General Cao had an idea.

He pointed to a grove of trees far ahead, and told them that they were plum trees. "Look! Let us hurry to reach the plum trees to enjoy them!"

The soldiers were very excited. They marched faster for the trees. They forgot about their thirst and fatigue.

However, the trees were not plum trees. But the soldiers reached their destination on time.

11

The Promise of the Plums

famous
military leader
soldiers
march
late summer
thirsty and tired
destination
guide
river
far away
idea
pointed
grove of trees
plum
hurry
trees
fatigue
reached
destination
on time

The Bad Horses

The Yellow Emperor, Huang Di, was a wise ruler in ancient China. The Chinese people recognize him as the forefather of the Chinese nation. They call themselves descendants of the Yellow Emperor.

One day, the Emperor went to the mountain to seek advice from God about how to govern a country. He met a stable boy on his way. During their conversation, Emperor Huang Di was impressed with the boy's cleverness. He decided to test the boy, asking him how to rule a country. The boy replied, "It is easy. Ruling a country is like taking care of a herd of horses; first, we need to identify the bad horses in the herd. These horses would lead the other horses astray."

The Emperor was even more impressed. He had learned a lesson from a little boy.

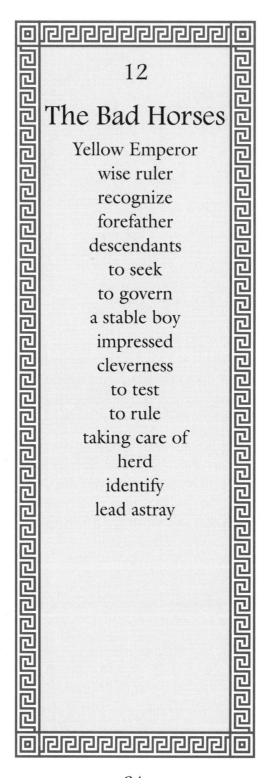

12

The Bad Horses

Yellow Emperor
wise ruler
recognize
forefather
descendants
to seek
to govern
a stable boy
impressed
cleverness
to test
to rule
taking care of
herd
identify
lead astray

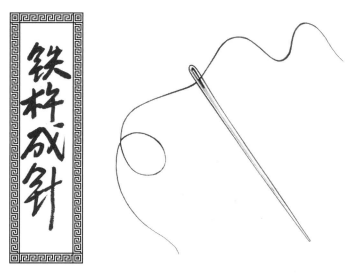

Making a Needle

Li Bai, a famous Chinese Poet, did not like to study when he was young. One day, he skipped school. He went to play by the river. He met an old woman there. The old woman was grinding a big iron rod. Li Bai was curious.

He asked, "Honorable Grandma, what are you doing?" The old woman replied, "Dear child, I am making a needle." Li Bai was surprised. "A needle? But how can you make a needle out of this huge iron rod?" he said. The old woman smiled and said, "You see, as long as I keep grinding, the rod will surely become a needle one day."

Li Bai was inspired. He vowed to study with the same kind of determination. He returned to school to study seriously and became the most famous poet in Chinese history. Children in China today are still required to recite his poems.

13

Making
a Needle

famous poet
young
skipped school
play
old woman
needle
grinding
iron rod
inspired
vowed
determination
seriously
children
required
recite

The Dragon Lover

O nce upon a time, a county officer was known for his love of dragons. His name was Yegong. He told everyone about his devotion to dragons.

Yegong decorated his house with images of dragons. He had dragons outside on his doors and windows. Inside, he had a big dragon mural. His dishes had dragon designs on them. His clothing was full of dragon prints.

The real dragon heard of Yegong's devotion to dragons and decided to pay him a visit. One day, it showed up at Yegong's house. Its head was in the window and its tail in the door.

"Hello, my friend!" the dragon said. Yegong was terrified and screamed, "Who are you, Evil Monster?" The dragon was surprised. It said, "I am the dragon you like so much. Don't you know me?"

Yegong begged the dragon to go away. He was not a true dragon lover after all.

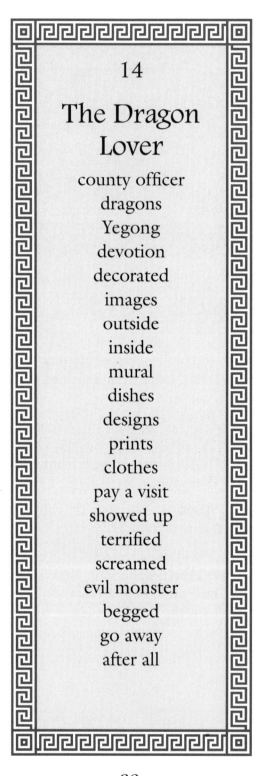

14

The Dragon Lover

county officer
dragons
Yegong
devotion
decorated
images
outside
inside
mural
dishes
designs
prints
clothes
pay a visit
showed up
terrified
screamed
evil monster
begged
go away
after all

The Walking Lesson

Shao Ling was a young man from the State of Yan. He was not very confident. He thought others were better than he was. When he looked at other people's clothing, their styles seemed much nicer. When he listened to other people's speech, their words seemed more elegant. One day, Shao Ling decided to learn the style of the people in the state of Zhao. They were especially known for their wonderful ways of walking.

Shao Ling moved to Zhao and observed and practiced how to walk like the people in Handan, the capital. He imitated old and young people, males and females. However, after a year's imitation, Shao Ling was not very successful. He failed to walk with the dignity of old people, the energy of young people, the masculinity of men, or the gentleness of women.

Worst of all, Shao Ling forgot the way he used to walk! Feeling utterly unsuccessful, Shao Ling crawled his way back home.

15

The Walking Lesson

Shao Ling
confident
others
clothing
styles
trendy
speech
elegant
state of Zhao
walking
observed and practiced
imitated
successful
dignity
energy
masculinity
gentleness
worst of all
crawled

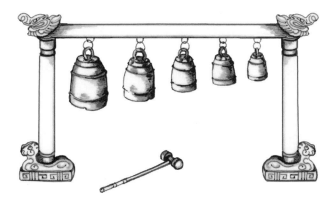

The Man and the Bell

A wealthy family named Fan had a wonderful set of Bian Zhong bells and many other valuables. However, the family got in trouble and they had to flee in the middle of the night to save their lives.

They abandoned their belongings, and people came to take away the things in their household. A poor man wanted to have their largest bell. He was afraid that others would also want the bell, so he tried to sneak it away. But it was too heavy.

The man went to get a hammer, thinking, "If I break the bell, I can carry away the pieces easily." When he struck the bell, it made a loud noise. The man covered his ears immediately. He hit the bell again, but he could not hear it, so he thought others could not hear it either, and they would not come to take it away. So he continued to strike the bell.

16

The Man and the Bell

wealthy family
Bian Zhong bells
trouble
flee
abandoned
poor man
largest bell
afraid
sneak it away
heavy
hammer
break
carry away
struck
noise
covered
others
take it away
continued
strike

Waiting for a Rabbit

Once upon a time, there was a farmer who wanted to have a good life, but he had to work in his field and take care of his crops to make a living.

One day, the farmer was resting by a tree near the field. A rabbit raced by, being chased by a hunter. The rabbit accidentally ran into the tree. It broke its neck and died instantly. The farmer was very happy to have the rabbit for dinner.

The farmer said to himself, "My luck is about to change. I do not need to work anymore. I can rest by this tree and wait to pick up a delicious meal every day."

From then on, the farmer stopped working in the field. Instead, he kept waiting by the tree, expecting another rabbit to hit the tree. But it didn't happen.

So the farmer never got a second free dinner. His field became worthless, and he became the laughing stock of his fellow country people.

17

Waiting for a Rabbit

good life
had to work
take care of
crops
a living
resting
rabbit
raced
chased
accidentally
ran into
broke
died
dinner
luck
anymore
delicious meal
waiting
expecting
happen
worthless
laughing stock

The Lost Sheep

One day, a shepherd lost a sheep. He asked his fellow villagers to help him find the sheep. Many went to help. Some went to the east; others went to the west. Still others went to the north and south, but the sheep was not found. In the evening, everyone returned home disappointed.

The shepherd told the village teacher about the event. The teacher asked why it was so difficult to find the sheep. The shepherd replied, "There were too many roads in the countryside. Although we sent many people to all directions, there were not enough people to investigate all the roads."

The teacher became very troubled and solemn for several days. His students asked him why he was sad. The teacher said, "The lost sheep reminds me of solving problems during the journey of learning. There are many roads in this journey. If people cannot focus on the problem, they will get lost and will never solve the problem."

18

The Lost Sheep

shepherd

sheep

villagers

find

east, west, north, south

problem

found

disappointed

village teacher

difficult

investigate

troubled and solemn

reminds

the journey of learning

focus

get lost

solve

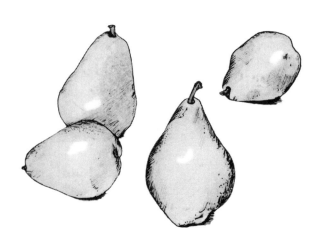

The Larger Pears

Long ago there was a little boy named Kong Rong. He was a genius. He was able to recite many poems at the age of four. He was very smart and also very kind.

Kong Rong had six brothers. Five of them were older. One day his father brought some pears for them. Instead of choosing a big one for himself, Kong Rong chose the larger pears, giving them to his older and younger brothers first. He saved the smallest one for himself.

His father observed this and asked him why he did so. Kong Rong replied, "I am younger than my older brothers; therefore, I ought to respect them, and let them have the larger pears; on the other hand, I am older than my younger brother. I ought to take care of him, and let him have a larger one." His father was very pleased with him.

Kong Rong became a famous poet when he grew up. However, people remember him mostly for his unselfish act as a little boy.

19

The Larger Pears

Long ago
genius
recite
smart and kind
brothers
father
pears
choosing
observed
older
respect
take care of
pleased
grew up
unselfish act

The Man and His Horse

Sai was an old man in Zhan Guo. He had many horses. One day he lost one of his horses. His neighbor felt sorry for him and tried to comfort him. However, Old Man Sai predicted that this was not necessarily an unfortunate event.

A few days later, Sai's horse came back with another horse. His neighbor was amazed that Sai's prophecy came true. Old Man Sai, on the other hand, was not thrilled. He said, "It might not be a blessing to gain a free horse."

Sai had a son who liked to ride. He fell in love with the new horse and rode it every day. One day he fell from the horse and broke his leg.

Instead of being upset, Old Man Sai saw this event as a blessing in disguise. A few days later, the Huns invaded China. Young men were drafted and went to war. Many of them died. However, Sai's son could not join the army because of his broken leg. The accident with the horse saved his life.

20

The Man and His Horse

Sai
horses
lost
felt sorry
predicted
not necessarily
unfortunate
came back
amazed
prophecy
not thrilled
blessing
to ride
broke
instead of
blessing in disguise
invaded
drafted
died
saved

The Clam and the Crane

A military advisor, Mr. Su, heard that the State of Zhao was going to attack the State of Yan. Mr. Su wanted to prevent the war, so he went to visit the Zhao Emperor. He told the emperor a story:

"Your Honor, on my way to see you this morning, I saw a crane and a clam on the river bank. The crane had poked its beak into the clam to get its meat; the clam had closed its shell tight, refusing to let go of the crane's beak. Neither of them would give up. They were determined to continue the fight and did not notice a fisherman who happened to walk by. He captured both the crane and the clam for dinner."

Su continued, "The most Honorable Emperor of Zhao, if you attack the State of Yan, Zhao and Yan would be like the crane and the clam, and the State of Qin would be the fisherman who would really benefit from the fighting."

Zhao Emperor was enlightened by the story and gave up the plan to attack Yan.

21

The Clam and the Crane

military advisor
Zhao
attack
Yan
told a story
a crane and a clam
poked its beak
closed
give up
fisherman
captured
Honorable Emperor
if
Zhao and Yan
like
State of Qin
benefit
enlightened
gave up

The Bamboo Artist

B amboo is a common theme in traditional Chinese arts. Bamboo symbolizes honesty and modesty, as it is hollow in the middle. Wen Tong, a famous artist, was especially known for painting bamboos.

Wen Tong planted bamboos all around his house, observing them day and night in all four seasons and all weather: spring, summer, winter, and fall, in sunshine or in rain. Whenever he painted bamboo, he never needed to make a sketch. He immediately painted the final picture as realistic as real bamboo in a short amount of time.

People admired Wen Tong's skills and wanted to learn from him. However, Wen Tong was modest and said he still could use much improvement. His good friend, Su Shi, another famous artist, told the people about Wen Tong's secret: Wen Tong knew the nature of bamboo so well that he always knew what he was going to paint before he put the image on paper. The secret of Wen Tong's success was his years of observing and learning the essence of bamboo.

22

The Bamboo Artist

Bamboo
theme
traditional
symbolizes
honesty
modesty
hollow
Wen Tong
observing
seasons
weather
whenever
sketch
final picture
realistic
admired
skills
modest
improvement
secret
nature of bamboo
image
essence

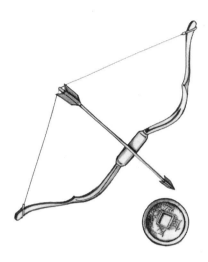

Practice

An archer was known for his skill with his bow and arrow. His townsfolk praised him often, and he was proud of himself too.

One day he showed off his skills in the market place by hitting a target easily. The crowds cheered for him. However, an old peddler who was selling oil was not impressed. The archer was offended by the old man's attitude. He asked the old man, "You don't think I'm very good, do you?"

The old man responded, "You are merely hitting a large target that is not moving. With practice, one can do anything. There is nothing extraordinary about it."

Without any further explanation, the old man put a gourd on the ground. He made a small hole in the gourd and then covered it with a Chinese coin that had a smaller hole in it. Holding his oil tank high, he poured the oil through the hole in the coin into the gourd. Then he picked up the coin to show the crowd. There was not a single drop of oil on the coin.

The crowd and the archer were amazed. Since then, the archer has stopped bragging about his skills, and he now practices even harder.

23

Practice

archer
townsfolk
praised
proud
showed off
market place
target
precision
cheered
peddler
oil
not impressed
offended
responded
with practice
extraordinary
explanation
gourd
hole
coin
oil tank
poured
crowd
drop
amazed
bragging
practices

The Reflection of the Snake

Mr. Yuegang and Mr. Ma were good friends. They visited each other often. One day, it occurred to Yuegang that Ma had not visited him for a long time. He went to Ma's house to see what was going on.

Ma was sick in bed at home. When asked why, Ma said, "Dear friend, when I went to eat at your house last time, I saw a snake in the wine cup. I did not want to drink the wine; however, you kept forcing it on me. I did not want to offend you and drank the wine. I have been sick since then."

Yuegang was puzzled to hear the story, knowing there was no snake in the wine. When he returned home, Yuegang saw a bow on the wall in the dining room. There was a painting of a snake on the bow. He then realized that the snake in the wine cup was actually a reflection of the painting on the bow.

Yuegang invited Ma back to his house. He poured some wine in the cup, and showed him the picture on the bow and the reflection of the snake. Ma's sickness was cured immediately.

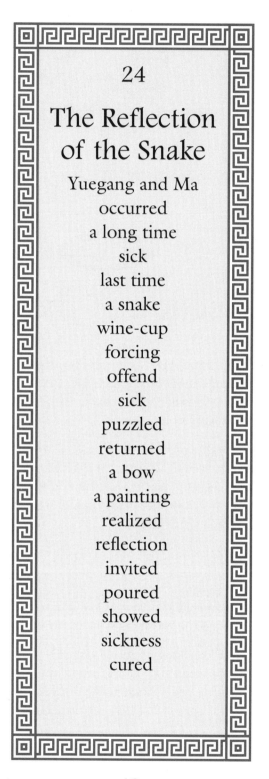

24

The Reflection of the Snake

Yuegang and Ma
occurred
a long time
sick
last time
a snake
wine-cup
forcing
offend
sick
puzzled
returned
a bow
a painting
realized
reflection
invited
poured
showed
sickness
cured

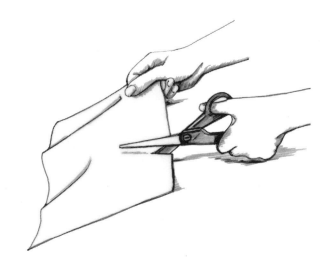

The Teacher's Mother

Mengzi was a famous Chinese teacher and Confucian philosopher. He was raised by his mother, who had great expectations of him. She moved their home three times for his benefit.

At first, they lived in a village. Mengzi often got into trouble, fighting with other boys. His mother thought the environment was not good for him and moved away. In the second village, they lived near a blacksmith. Mengzi acted like the uneducated blacksmith. His mother moved near a cemetery. Mengzi's mother found him imitating the grave diggers. Finally, she moved to a village and lived by a school. Mengzi started to imitate the teacher by playing school. His mother was pleased.

One day, however, Mengzi didn't want to go to school anymore. His mother taught him a lesson. She cut the fabric she was weaving, "I am weaving the fabric to make a garment but the garment will never be made if I stop making the fabric. Being successful in studies is like making a garment, you can't stop halfway."

Mengzi listened to his mother, went back to school, and studied hard. He became one of the greatest Chinese philosophers.

25

The Teacher's Mother

philosopher
raised
great expectations
moved
village
fights
blacksmith
imitated
cemetery
school
teacher
anymore
taught a lesson
cut fabric
weave
garment
stop
halfway
went back
became

PART 2

1 The Snake with Feet

Dictation

One day,   a rich man   gave his servants
a bottle of wine.

He told them   to share it.

There were   many servants,   but not much wine.

The servants decided   to play a game.

They decided   to draw snakes.

The first one   to finish   would win.

Servant Wang   finished first.

However,   he decided   to add feet.

While Servant Wang   was adding feet,   Servant Li finished.

Wang   did not drink   the wine.

Comprehension Questions

Who gave the wine?

How much wine did he give?

Who did he give it to?

What did he tell them?

What did the servants decide?

Who finished first?

What did Wang decide to do?

When did Li finish?

Who won the bottle of wine?

Why did he win?

2 The Spear and the Shield

Dictation

Different regions   fought each other   in ancient times.

A weapons seller   tried to sell   his weapons.

He held   his spear   high in the air.

"These spears   can penetrate   the strongest shields,"
he said.

Then the man   held the shield   high in the air.

"These are   the strongest shields   in the world,"
he said.

A listener shouted,   "What happens   if your spears
attack your shields?"

The merchant   was speechless.

He did not know   what to say.

Comprehension Questions

What happened in ancient times?

Who tried to sell weapons?

What did he hold high in the air?

What can the spears penetrate?

What did he do with the shield?

What did he say about the shield?

Who shouted at him?

What did he shout?

What did the merchant say?

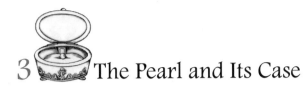

3 The Pearl and Its Case

Dictation

A merchant   had a valuable pearl.

He tried   to sell it   for a high price.

No one   wanted to spend   a lot of money.

He decided   to make   a beautiful case
for the pearl.

He put   the pearl inside   and displayed it   in its case.

The display   looked beautiful.

A buyer   was attracted   to the beautiful display.

He bought   the pearl   and its case.

He gave   the pearl back   to the merchant.

He walked away   with the case.

Comprehension Questions

What did the merchant have?

What did he want to do with the pearl?

Who bought the pearl?

What did he make?

Where did he put the pearl?

How did the display look?

What did he buy?

Who did he give the pearl to?

Where did he go with the case?

4 Playing Music to a Cow

Dictation

A famous musician   played the Chinese zither.

He was known   for his great skill.

Everyone loved   his music.

However,   sometimes his behavior   seemed silly.

One day   he was traveling   in the countryside.

He saw   a cow   eating grass.

He started to play   his zither   in front of the cow.

The cow   was not interested   in the music.

The cow   kept on eating   and behaving like a cow.

The musician   did not understand   the cow's behavior.

Comprehension Questions

What did the musician play?

What was he known for?

Who loved his music?

How was his behavior sometimes?

Where was he traveling?

What did he see?

What did he start to do?

How did the cow feel?

What did the cow continue to do?

What did the musician think?

5   The Dragons without Eyes

Dictations

Zhang was   a famous artist.

The emperor   liked his paintings   very much.

He asked Zhang   to paint four dragons   for the temple.

Zhang finished   the painting   in three days.

The dragons   looked very real.

There were   no eyes   on the dragons.

He said,   "If I paint eyes,   the dragons   will fly away."

Nobody   believed him,   so he told them   to come and watch.

When he finished   painting the eyes,   two dragons came to life   and flew away.

Comprehension Questions

Who liked Zhang's paintings?

How much did he like them?

How many dragons did Zhang paint?

Where did he paint them?

How did the dragons look?

How many eyes did the dragons have?

What did Zhang say about the eyes?

Who believed him?

What did he tell them?

What happened when he painted the eyes?

6 The Lost Sword

Dictation

A man was crossing the Yangtze River.

The river is famous for its beautiful scenery.

The man stood by the edge of the boat.

He wanted to enjoy the scenery.

His sword accidentally fell into the water.

He marked a spot on the boat.

A fellow traveler urged him to jump in the river.

The man said, "When we reach the shore
I will jump in at this spot."

I will find the sword.

Comprehension Questions

What was the man doing?

Why is the river famous?

Where did the man stand?

Why did he stand there?

What happened to his sword?

What did the man do?

What did the fellow traveler say?

What did the man say?

What did he find?

7 The Money Sign

Dictation

People used gold and silver coins as money.

However, they did not deposit their money in banks.

A man inherited three hundred pieces of silver.

He decided to hide the coins.

He was afraid someone might steal the coins.

He put up a sign.

It said, "There is no money in this spot."

A neighbor stole the money.

He put up a sign.

It said, "Your neighbor did not steal the money."

Comprehension Questions

What kind of coins did people use?

How many banks were there?

What did the man inherit?

How many pieces of silver did he get?

What did he put up.

What did it say?

Who stole the money?

What did he do?

Monkey Math

Dictation

Once there was   a man   who loved monkeys.

He kept   many monkeys   as pets.

It was expensive   to keep   the monkeys.

They required   lots of bananas   and fruit.

One day   he said,   "I am getting poor."

I can give   only three bananas   in the morning and four at night."

The monkeys   protested.

The man said,   "I will sacrifice."

"I will give four   in the morning   and three at night."

The monkeys   accepted his proposal.

Comprehension Questions

What did the man love?

What did he do with the monkeys?

How much did it cost to keep the monkeys?

What did the monkeys require?

What did he tell the monkeys?

How many bananas could he give?

What did the monkeys do?

What did the man say?

How many bananas would he give?

What did the monkeys do?

9 The Man Buying Shoes

Dictation

One day, Zheng wanted to buy a pair of shoes.

He measured his feet with a string.

After traveling twenty miles he arrived at the shoe shop.

It took him a long time to select the shoes.

He realized he had left the string at home.

He returned home to get the string.

By the time he came back, the shop was closed.

People asked why he didn't try the shoes on his feet?

Zheng said, "I know the measurement of the string, but I don't know the measurement of my feet."

Comprehension Questions

What did Zheng want to do?

What did he measure?

How did he measure?

How far did he go?

Where did he go?

How long did it take him to select the shoes?

What did he realize?

Where did he go?

What did he find when he came back?

What did people ask?

What did he tell people?

10 The Fox and the Tiger

Dictation

The tiger   was the King   of the Forest.

One day   he caught   a fox.

The fox   was very clever.

The fox said,   "If you eat me,   God will punish you."

The tiger   was very doubtful,   so the fox said,
"Let us   walk together.   You walk behind."

You will see   the animals   are terrified of me."

They walked   into the forest.

All the animals   fled immediately.

The fox   tricked the tiger   and the tiger
lost a meal.

Comprehension Questions

Who was the King of the Forest?

What did he catch?

Who was very clever?

What did the fox say?

Who would punish the tiger?

Who was very doubtful.

What did the fox tell the tiger?

Where did they go?

What happened?

11 The Promise of the Plums

Dictation

General Cao was a famous military leader.

Once he led his soldiers on a long march.

The soldiers became very thirsty and tired.

The guide said the river was still very far away.

General Cao told the troops to look at a grove of trees.

He said they were plum trees.

The soldiers were very excited.

They marched faster for the plum trees.

However, the trees were not plum trees.

The soldiers reached their destination on time.

Comprehension Questions

Who was General Cao?

Who did he lead?

What kind of march was it?

What happened to the soldiers?

What did the guide say?

What did the general tell the soldiers?

How did the soldiers feel?

What did they do?

What did they reach?

12 The Bad Horses

Dictation

The Yellow Emperor, Huang Di, was a wise ruler in ancient China.

The Chinese people recognize him as the forefather of the Chinese nation.

One day the emperor went to the mountain to ask God for advice.

He wanted advice on how to govern a country.

He met a stable boy on the way.

The emperor was impressed with the boy's cleverness.

The boy said ruling a country is like taking care of horses.

We need to identify the bad horses in the herd.

He said the bad horses would lead the others astray.

Comprehension Questions

Who was Huang Di?

What do the Chinese people think about him?

Where did the emperor go one day?

What did he want?

Who did he meet?

Why did the boy impress him?

What did he tell the emperor?

What did the emperor need to do?

What would the bad horses do?

13 Making a Needle

Dictation

Li Bai is   a famous   Chinese poet.

He did not like   to study   when he was young.

One day   he skipped school   and went to the river.

He met   an old woman there.

She was grinding   a big iron rod.

Li Bai asked,   "What are you doing?"

She replied,   "I am making   a needle."

Li Bai   was surprised.

The old woman said   the rod would become   a needle some day.

Li Bai was inspired,   and he returned   to school.

Comprehension Questions

Who is Li Bai?

What did he not like to do?

What did he do one day?

Where did he go?

Who did he meet there?

What was she doing?

What did Li Bai ask?

How did she reply?

How did Li Bai feel?

What did he do?

14 The Dragon Lover

Dictation

A county officer   named Yegong   loved dragons.

He told everyone   about his devotion   to dragons.

He decorated   his house   with images   of dragons.

The real dragon   heard about   Yegong's devotion
to dragons.

He decided   to pay him   a visit.

One day   he showed up   at Yegong's house.

The dragon said,   "Hello, my friend!"

Yegong was terrified   and he screamed.

He begged the dragon   to go away.

He was not   a true dragon lover   after all.

Comprehension Questions

What did the county officer love?

What was his name?

Who did he tell about his devotion?

What did he decorate?

What kind of decorations did he have?

Who heard about Yegong's devotion.

What did he decide to do?

What did he call out?

How did Yegong react?

What did he ask the dragon?

15 The Walking Lesson

Dictation

Shao Ling was from the state of Yan.

He thought others were better than he was.

He decided to learn the style of the people of Zhao.

The Zhao people were known for their way of walking.

Shao Ling moved to Zhao.

He observed and practiced how to walk like the people in Handan.

However after a year of imitating them, he was not very successful.

Shao Ling forgot the way he used to walk.

He crawled his way back home.

Comprehension Questions

Where did Shao Ling come from?

How did he feel about himself?

What did he decide to do?

Who were known for their style of walking?

Where did Shao Ling go?

What did he do there?

How well did he do?

What did he forget?

How did he get back home?

16 The Man and the Bell

Dictation

The Fan family had a wonderful set of bells.

The family got in trouble and had to flee to save their lives.

They abandoned their belongings.

People came to take them away.

A poor man wanted the largest bell.

It was too heavy to carry away.

The man went to get a hammer.

When he struck the bell, it made a loud noise.

He covered his ears immediately and he couldn't hear the bell.

He thought others could not hear the bell.

Comprehension Questions

What did the Fan family have?

Why did they have to flee?

What did they abandon?

What did people do?

Who wanted the largest bell?

How heavy was the bell?

What did the man get?

What happened when he struck the bell?

What did he do?

What did he think?

17 Waiting for a Rabbit

Dictation

There was a farmer   who wanted   a good life.

He had to   take care of   his crops   to make a living.

One day   he was resting   by a tree.

A rabbit   was being chased   by a hunter.

It ran into the tree   and broke its neck.

The farmer   had the rabbit   for dinner.

He decided   to rest by the tree   every day   and get a delicious dinner.

However,   nothing happened   and he never got a second dinner.

His field   became worthless   and he became the laughing stock   of the village.

Comprehension Questions

What did the farmer want to have?

What did he have to do?

Who was chasing the rabbit?

What happened to the rabbit?

What did the farmer get?

What did he decide to do?

Where did he do it?

What happened?

What happened to his field?

What did he become?

18 The Lost Sheep

Dictation

One day   a shepherd   lost a sheep.

He asked his villagers   to help him   find the sheep.

In the evening   they returned home   disappointed.

The shepherd   told the village teacher
about the lost   sheep.

The teacher asked   why it was difficult   to find the sheep.

The shepherd said   there were   too many roads
in the countryside.

The teacher became   very troubled
and his students   asked him   why he was sad.

He said   the lost sheep   reminded him
of the journey   of learning.

There are   many roads   on the journey   of learning.

If people cannot focus   on the problem,   they will
never solve it.

Comprehension Questions

What did the shepherd lose?

What did he ask the villagers?

When did they return home?

How did they feel?

Who told the village teacher about the sheep?

What did the teacher ask?

What did the shepherd say?

How did the teacher feel?

What did he tell his students?

19  The Larger Pears

Dictation

Kong Rong   was a genius.

At the age of four   he was able   to recite
many poems.

He was very smart   and also very kind.

One day   his father brought   some pears   for him
and his six brothers.

He gave his brothers   the larger pears.

He kept the smallest one   for himself.

His father asked him   why he did that.

Kong Rong replied that   he should respect
his older brothers.

He said   he should take care of   his younger brother.

His father   was very pleased   with his answer.

Comprehension Questions

What kind of person was Kong Rong?

What could he do at the age of four?

What did his father bring?

Who were the pears for?

How many brothers did Kong Rong have?

What did King Rong do with the pears?

Which pears did he give to his brothers?

Which pear did he keep for himself?

What did his father ask?

What did Kong Rong say to his father?

20 The Man and His Horse

Dictation

Sai was   an old man   who lived in Zhan Guo.

One day   he lost one of his horses,   and his neighbor
felt sorry for him.

Sai did not think   this was   an unfortunate event.

One day   the horse came back   with another horse.

His neighbor was amazed,   but Old Man Sai
was not thrilled.

Sai had a son   who fell in love   with the new horse.

One day   Sai's son   fell off the new horse
and broke his leg,   but Sai was not upset.

A few days later   the Huns invaded China,
and many young men   went to war.

Sai's son   could not go   because of   his broken leg.

The accident with the horse   saved his son's life.

Comprehension Questions

Where did old Sai live?

What did he lose one day?

Who tried to comfort him?

What did Sai think?

Who came back with the horse?

How did the neighbor and Sai feel?

What happened to Sai's son?

How did Sai feel then?

What did the Huns do, and what happened then?

21 The Clam and the Crane

Dictation

Mr. Su was a military advisor.

He heard that Zhao was going to attack Yan.

He wanted to prevent war, so he told
the Zhao emperor a story.

A crane had poked its beak into a clam.

The clam had closed its shell on the crane's beak.

Neither of them would give up so they continued
to fight.

A fisherman captured both the crane and the clam.

Su told the emperor, if he attacked Yan, Qin would be
like the fisherman.

Qin would benefit from the fighting.

The emperor was enlightened by the story
and gave up his plan to attack Yan.

Comprehension Questions

Who was Mr. Su?

What did he hear?

What did he tell the emperor?

What did the crane do?

What did the clam do?

Who continued to fight?

Who captured them?

What did Su tell the emperor?

How did the emperor react?

22 The Bamboo Artist

Dictation

Bamboo is a common theme in traditional Chinese arts.

Bamboo symbolizes honesty and modesty.

Wen Tong was a famous artist who was known for painting bamboo.

He planted them all around his house.

He observed them day and night in all four seasons.

Whenever he painted bamboo, he never needed to make a sketch.

He immediately painted the final picture in a short amount of time.

People admired his skills and wanted to learn from him.

His friend told them Wen Tong's secret.

Wen Tong knew what he was going to paint before he put the image on paper.

Comprehension Questions

What is a common theme in traditional Chinese arts?

What does bamboo symbolize?

Who was Wen Tong?

What was he known for?

Where did he plant bamboo?

When did he observe the bamboo?

How long did it take him to paint a picture of bamboo?

Who wanted to learn from him?

Who told them his secret, and what was it?

23 Practice

Dictation

An archer was known for his skill with his bow and arrow.

One day he showed off his skill in the market place.

He hit the target easily and the crowds cheered.

An old peddler was not impressed.

The archer was offended by the old man's attitude.

The old man said he was merely hitting a target that was not moving.

He said that with practice one can do anything.

He put a hole in a gourd and covered it with a coin that had a hole.

He poured oil through the coin into the gourd.

There was not a single drop of oil on the coin.

Comprehension Questions

Who was known for his skill with a bow and arrow?

Where did he show off his skill?

How well did he do, and who cheered?

Who offended the archer?

What did the old man say?

What did the old man do with the gourd?

What kind of coin did he use to cover the hole?

What did he do then?

What happened?

24 The Reflection of the Snake

Dictation

Mr. Yuegang and Mr. Ma visited each other often.

For a long time, Ma had not visited Yuegang.

Yuegang went to see Ma.

Ma explained that he saw a snake in his wine cup at Yuegang's house, and it made him sick.

Yuegang was puzzled because he knew there was no snake in the wine.

When he went home he saw a bow hanging on the wall.

On it was a painting of a snake.

He realized that Ma had seen a reflection.

He invited Ma to return and showed him the reflection of the snake.

Ma's sickness was cured immediately.

Comprehension Questions

Who visited each other often?

Who had not visited Yuegang for a long time?

Where did Yuegang go?

What did Ma explain?

How did Yuegang feel, and why did he feel that way?

What did he see when he went home?

Where was the painting?

What did Yuegang realize?

What did he do then and what happened to Ma?

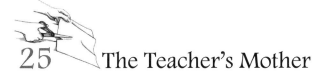

25 The Teacher's Mother

Dictation

Mengzi was   a famous teacher   and Confucian philosopher.

He was raised   by his mother.

She moved their home   three times.

At first   they lived in a village,   but Mengzi got into fights.

They moved   near a blacksmith,   but Mengzi acted like a blacksmith.

They moved   near a cemetery,   but Mengzi imitated the grave diggers.

They moved   near a school   and Mengzi acted like a school teacher.

One day   he did not want   to go to school.

His mother   taught him a lesson   with some fabric she was weaving.

She showed him   that you can't be successful   at studies if you stop halfway.

Comprehension Questions

Who was Mengzi?

Who raised him?

How many times did they move?

What happened in the first village?

What happened when they lived near the blacksmith?

What happened when they lived near a cemetery?

When they moved near a school what happened?

What happened one day?

What did his mother do?

What did she show him?

PART 3

Discussion Questions for the Tales

Note: The questions below are meant only to stimulate and initiate discussion of the stories. The ensuing discussion could certainly be guided by other questions such as "Did you like the story?" "Do you know others like it?"

In general, the first question relates to the factual content of the story, and the second question relates to the purpose of the story. In general, most of the stories can be seen as stories to entertain or stories to teach with an implied moral. The morals have been purposefully omitted from the story to stimulate thinking and discussing.

1. The Snake with Feet

    A. Why do you think Wang decided to add feet?

    B. What lesson does this story teach?

2. The Spear and the Shield

    A. How would you answer the listener's question?

    B. What lesson does this story teach?

3. The Pearl and Its Case

    A. Why did the buyer return the pearl?

    B. Did the seller learn anything?

4. Playing Music to a Cow

    A. Why did the musician play his zither for the cow?

    B. What did the musician learn from this experience?

5. The Dragons without Eyes

    A. What happened when Zhang gave the dragons eyes?

    B. What is the purpose of this story?

6. The Lost Sword

    A. Why didn't the man jump into the water?

    B. What lesson does this story teach?

7. The Money Sign

    A. Who was smarter, the man or his neighbor?

    B. Why did these men put up signs?

8. Monkey Math

    A. How did the man trick the monkeys?

    B. Why is this called "monkey math?"

9. The Man Buying Shoes

    A. What was wrong with the man's thinking?

    B. Is this story for entertainment or instruction?

10. The Fox and the Tiger

    A. How did the fox trick the tiger?

    B. Is there a lesson in this story? If so, what is the lesson?

11. The Promise of the Plums

    A. Why did the soldiers hurry to reach the plums?

    B. The General tricked his soldiers. Was that a good thing to do?

12. The Bad Horses

    A. Why did the boy talk to the emperor about horses?

    B. Do you agree with the boy's advice to the emperor?

13. Making a Needle

    A. How did Li Bai meet the old woman?

    B. What is the lesson the old woman taught?

14. The Dragon Lover

    A. How did the man show his love for dragons?

    B. Is there a lesson in this story?

15. The Walking Lesson

    A. Why did Shao Ling decide to go to Zhao?

    B. What is the moral of this story?

16. The Man and the Bell

    A. Why did the man decide to break the bell?

    B. Why was his decision a bad idea?

17. Waiting for a Rabbit

    A. Why did the man decide to wait for another rabbit?

    B. What can we learn from this story?

18. The Lost Sheep

    A. Why did the villagers fail to find the lost sheep?

    B. What lesson did the teacher tell his students?

19. The Larger Pears

    A. Why did Kong Rong take the smallest pear?

    B. Would you do what Kong Rong did?

20. The Man and His Horse

    A. The old man did not get upset about the lost horse. Why?

    B. Is there a lesson in this story? If so, what is the lesson?

21. The Clam and the Crane

    A. Why do many stories have animals as characters?

    B. What is the moral of this story?

22. The Bamboo Artist

    A. How did Wen Tong become good at drawing bamboo?

    B. What is the lesson to be learned?

23. Practice

    A. Why did the old man teach the archer a lesson?

    B. What lesson did the archer learn?

24. The Reflection of the Snake

    A. Why did Mr. Ma become sick?

    B. What does this story say about sickness and health?

25. The Teacher's Mother

    A. Why did the mother move so often?

    B. Is there a lesson to be learned from this story? If so, what is the lesson?

Background Information

A Brief Timeline

Ancient
> Xia: ca. 2200–ca. 1600 BCE
>
> Shang: ca. 1600–ca. 1040 BCE
>
> Western Zhou: ca. 1100–771 BCE
>
> Eastern Zhou: The Spring/Autumn Period and Warring States: 770–221 BCE

Imperial
> Qin: 221–206 BCE
>
> Han: 206 BCE–220 CE
>
> The Three Kingdoms (Wei, Shu, Wu) 220–280
>
> Jin: 265–420
>
> Nanbei Dynasties: 316–589
>
> Sui : 589–618
>
> Tang: 618–907
>
> Five Dynasties and Ten Kingdoms: 907–960
>
> Northern and Southern Song: 960–1279
>
> Yuan: 1279–1368
>
> Ming: 1368–1644
>
> Qing: 1644–1911

Modern
> Republic of China 1912–1949
>
> People's Republic of China 1949–present

Adapted from: www-chaos.umd.edu/history/toc.html and en.wikipedia.org/wiki/Ancient_China.

Historical and Cultural Background

These stories are famous in China. Most of them were recorded in classic Chinese in different historical periods, as early as the 3rd century, BCE. Some of the names of the characters in the stories are the original names, while others that did not have specific names were invented by the author.

1. The Snake with Feet

This story happened in the Spring-Autumn and Warring State period (770–221 BCE). Chu was a region in the southern part of China that is different from northern China in its geography, climate, food (Southern Chinese eat more rice while northern Chinese eat more noodles), culture, and language. And there are more snakes in the south. The snake is the sixth among the 12 Chinese Zodiac animal symbols. The snake is also called little dragon in the Zodiac. These 12 animals are the rat, ox, tiger, rabbit, dragon, snake, horse, sheep, monkey, rooster, dog, and pig. Wine is very popular in China both in northern and southern China throughout history. It always accompanies banquets and celebrations.

2. The Spear and the Shield

This story takes place in the Spring-Autumn and Warring State period (770–221 BCE). A famous Chinese book, *The Art of War*, written in the 6th century, CE, explained many important principles of warfare. Chinese martial arts have been important even before gunpowder was used in war. It has a long history of over 3,000 years. Traditional Chinese martial arts use fists or weaponry in self-defense or fighting. Chinese martial arts emphasize training physically and mentally. People need to discipline their bodies physically. They also need to train their minds and will. The inner virtue of martial arts is as important as the physical skills. Humility, loyalty, respect, endurance, righteousness, and courage are important qualities for successful martial artists.

3. The Pearl and Its Case

This story is about a merchant selling a precious pearl. The word for sell is *mai* in Chinese. The word for business in Chinese is *Mai Mai*. These two "mai" are differentiated by their tones, as Chinese is a tonal language. The first "mai" is the third tone and the second "mai" is the fourth tone. The first "mai" means to buy; hence, "business" in Chinese literally means "buy and sell," just as a successful business transaction involves both buying ad selling. The Chinese have been doing international business as early as the 1st century. The Silk Road is a famous ancient trade route between China and the West. Chinese silk, spice, and culture were exported to the Middle East and Europe. Meanwhile, Buddhism and elements of western culture were transmitted to China through the Silk Road. Marco Polo traveled on the Silk Road to China in the 13th century.

4. Playing Music to a Cow

The Zither is a traditional Chinese music instrument. It has a history of over 3,000 years. It is a string instrument. Its strings are made of silk. There are many kinds of zither instruments. The Gu Qin is the kind that was favored by scholars and literati in history. Its music was classified as one of the Masterpieces of the Oral and Intangible Heritage of Humanity by UNESCO (United Nations Educational, Scientific, and Cultural Organization). Traditional Chinese culture prizes the four arts, "music, chess, calligraphy, and painting," as the four skills that an educated person should have. Music is very important to the cultivation of virtue and spirit in Chinese philosophical thought. Confucius, along with many other famous Chinese writers, was a skilled Gu Qin player.

5. The Dragons without Eyes

The great artist, Zhang, lived during the Nanbei Dynasties (316–589 CE). During this period, the Huns invaded China. The Chinese empire was split into the North and South empires, and many small states were established. Also during this period, Buddhism was introduced to China from India. Since then, Buddhism has become a popular religion in China. Liang Wu Di, an emperor in Liang, was a devoted believer of Buddhism. There were many Buddhist temples in Nanjing, the capital of Liang at that time. However, many of the temples were destroyed in later years. Nanjing served as capital for several other dynasties in China, including the Republic of China in 1911. Today Nanjing is the capital of Jiangsu province. It is in the southeastern part of China. It is a beautiful place to visit.

6. The Lost Sword

This story took place on a river in southern China. There are two major rivers in China: the Yellow River in the north and the Yangtze River in the south. The Yangtze River is also called the Long River. It is the third longest river in the world and the longest river in China. It originates from the Tibetan plateau, flows eastward across China toward the Pacific Ocean. The Yangtze River divides China into northern and southern parts. The northern Chinese are generally taller. They like to eat noodles and pasta dishes; the southern Chinese are generally shorter in stature, and they favor rice and rice products. Since the 1990s, China has been constructing the largest dam in the world on the Yangtze River. This project flooded many regions in the upper section of the Yangtze River to generate electricity and control floods in the lower parts. The Three Gorges is one of the most beautiful regions on the Yangtze River in the upper section of Yangtze. Many poems were written about the Three Gorges in Chinese classical literature. It will be flooded once the dam is completed. The dam is located in Sichuan Province in southwest China.

7. The Money Sign

In this story, the name "Little Er" literally means "Little Number two." It's a general and popular name like John Doe in English.

In ancient China, people used gold, silver, and copper for money. Money came in the shape of semi-circle nuggets. Silver nuggets were most common, and there were gold nuggets too. Pot Stickers, also called Jiao Zi, a popular Chinese food, were made in the same shape as the silver nuggets. Pot stickers are the most traditional Chinese holiday food. People eat pot stickers on Chinese New Year because they believe pot stickers, in the shape of silver nuggets, may bring them good fortune. Sometimes people put coins in the pot stickers randomly. If a person bites into the pot stickers that contain the coins, they will be the luckiest one. The silver nugget is a common theme in Chinese arts and crafts. Many necklaces and bracelets have the shape of a silver nugget design.

China also invented paper money. Paper money was circulated as early as the ninth century. When Marco Polo came to China later in the thirteenth century, he was fascinated with the idea and practice of people using paper money. He recounted this observation in his book *Travels of Marco Polo*.

8. Monkey Math

Although monkeys are portrayed as stupid in this story, they are favorable animals in Chinese culture. They are considered to be very smart. A famous Chinese novel, *Journey to the West*, stars a monkey named Monkey King or Sun Wukong. Money King accompanied his master, a monk, on his journey to the West to find the Holy Scriptures. Throughout the journey, Monkey King protected his master with his wit, courage, and skills. Money King is a beloved figure among Chinese people, young and old. Monkey King appears in Chinese drama with a painted mask of a monkey. His personality is characterized by the virtues of justice, righteousness, honesty, and loyalty.

9. The Man Buying Shoes

This story took place in the region of Zheng (Zheng is also a common Chinese name) in the Spring and Autumn and Warring State periods (770–221 BCE). During that time, China was divided into several smaller states. These states were constantly in diplomatic negotiations and fighting with each other. Eventually, the state of Qin conquered the rest of the regions and united China. The location of the state of Zheng is in the central part of China. It is in the current Henan Province. Due to its location, Zheng was prosperous in its commerce, as it borders several other states. Today Zhengzhou is the capital of Henan Province. It is where the two main railroads, North-South and East-West, connect with each other. It is one of the busiest commercial and transportation centers in China.

10. The Fox and the Tiger

In Chinese culture, the tiger is considered as the King of the Forest. It is said that the stripes on Tigers' forehead indicate the Chinese word *Wang*, which means "king." The Tiger is also a common motif in traditional Chinese painting. It is a symbol of power and good fortune. There are different kinds of tigers in China. Siberian tigers live in the northeastern part of China; the South China tigers live in southern and eastern China. Both are endangered species. In traditional Chinese medicine, different parts of the tiger are considered precious and powerful medicine for various ailments. Poachers capture tigers for their fur and body parts. Also, Tiger Balm is a famous Asian trademark for a type of ointment that cures muscle pains, headaches, insect bites, stuffy nose, and itchiness.

11. The Promise of the Plums

General Chao (155–220 CE), known by Chinese people as Chao Chao, was a renowned historical figure in Chinese history. He was a high government official in the Eastern Han Dynasty. He also laid the foundation for his son to later establish the state of Wei in the northern part of China during the Three Kingdom period. The other two kingdoms were Shu in southwestern China and Wu in southeastern China.

Chao Chao's grandfather was a eunuch in the Imperial Palace. Chao Chao was a military genius and strategist. He was also known to be very kind to his officers. A famous Chinese classic novel, *The Legend of the Three Kingdoms*, was about Chao Chao and his contemporaries. The novel portrayed Chao Chao as a cruel and cunning person. In Chinese opera, the stories about Chao Chao are a common theme. The character for Chao Chao always wears a white painted mask to indicate his cunning character. However, historically, Chao Chao was considered a successful politician. He was also a brilliant poet. His poems are about military life and life in general, and the language of his poetry is beautiful yet powerful.

12. The Bad Horses

The Yellow Emperor (Huang Di) is a legendary hero and king in Chinese mythology. It is said he reigned from 2697 BCE to 2598 BCE. The Han Chinese, the majority ethnic group of Chinese, consider themselves as descendants of the Yellow Emperor. The Yellow Emperor contributed much to Chinese culture. It is said that he invented the basic principles in traditional Chinese medicine. His wife was the inventor of sericulture—making silk from silk worms. It is also said that his minister, Cang Ji, was the inventor of Chinese characters. The Yellow Emperor was credited with the invention of the Gu Qin—a classical Chinese music instrument, as well as the magical compass chariot. The chariot could calculate the distance it traveled. It also had a carved wooden person pointing his hand to the south at all times. It was a technological marvel. The tomb of the Yellow Emperor is a tourist attraction in Shang Xi Province in today's China. Every year, Chinese people from all over the world visit his tomb to pay their respects.

13. Making a Needle

This story is about Li Bai as a child. Li Bai (701–762 CE) was the most famous poet in Chinese history. He was born in the Tang Dynasty, when China was very strong economically, socially, and politically. He was born of a wealthy family and grew up in southwestern China. He traveled to many places during his youth, including the eastern provinces in China. He also worked in the Imperial Academy for a while.

Li Bai was nicknamed Poet Immortal because of the creative, bold images in his poems. The emperor liked his poetry very much. He asked Li Bai to write many poems. Li Bai's favorite topics are the moon, friendship, nature, and wine. He wrote many poems. More than a thousand were left for people to enjoy today.

14. The Dragon Lover

This story talks about a legendary animal, the dragon. The dragon is a mythological figure in many parts of the world, but it is a beloved symbol in Chinese culture. Chinese people refer to themselves as "descendants of the dragon." Unlike in western culture, where dragons are often associated with evil and violence, dragons are usually associated with power and good luck in Chinese culture. The dragon was the symbol for imperial power in Chinese history. It is also a common theme in Chinese arts and crafts.

The physical appearance of the dragon embodies nine other kinds of animals. It is said that the dragon has a camel head, deer horns, fish scales, a snake body, a clam belly, cow ears, rabbit eyes, tiger paws, and eagle claws. It is also said there are 117 scales on the dragon with 81 male-type scales and 36 female-type scales, which gives the dragon a balanced personality. Dragons are in charge of the weather, the ocean, the earth, and the sky.

15. The Walking Lesson

The story took place during the Spring-Autumn and Warring State period (770–221 BC). The young man from Yan in the story went to learn how to walk in the state of Zhao. Even though Yan and Zhao were both in China, they were different regions. During this period, China was not united. There were many different regions with different cultures. They used different languages, money systems, and measurement systems. Zhao and Yan were almost like two different countries.

16. The Man and the Bell

This story tells about a foolish man trying to steal a bronze bell in the Spring-Autumn and Warring State Period (770–221 BCE). Bronze art, tools, and weapons were used in China as early as 1500 BCE. Only royalty and wealthy families had bronze vessels. Bronze music instruments and vessels were also common burial artifacts. There are many Chinese bronze artifacts from this period in museums all over the world today.

The Ancient Chinese used bronze bells as percussion instruments in music. The bronze bells normally came as a set. There could be as many as 65 bells to a set. They were played at festival settings or religious ceremonies. Ancient Chinese bronze bells also had writings on them. These writings were mainly music theories. The Ancient Chinese viewed music not as a form of entertainment or amusement, but as a means to cultivate virtue and calm the spirit.

17. Waiting for a Rabbit

There is a big difference between urban life and rural life in Chinese culture. This story is set in the countryside. China for the most part is an agricultural society, and most Chinese live in the countryside. Many families were farmers for generations. Even now, farmers generally have limited access and resources to infrastructure, education, health care, entertainment, and social mobility compared to people in the cities.

The living standard in the city is normally higher than that of the countryside. City life is more desirable than life in the countryside. Many people from the countryside wish to be able to work and permanently reside in the cities. Many rural families try to marry their daughters into city families. Young people from the countryside often study hard to pass the college entrance examination to attend colleges and universities. When they graduate, they have a better chance to find a job in the city.

18. The Lost Sheep

This story tells about a lost sheep on a country road. The word for road in Chinese is *lu*. It is also called dao. "Dao" means "road," and it also means "truth" and "the way." The word "Taoism" is "Daoism" in Chinese.

Taoism is a major philosophy and religion. It argues that there is a "way" in the operation and function of the universe. In order for people to have peace, they should harmonize themselves with " the Way." There is also a natural way to everyday life. In order for people to have a good life, they should try to "go with the flow" and follow the natural way of life. According Taoism, living a good life is learning to find the truth, the way.

19. The Larger Pears

Kong Rong (153–208) was a direct descendant of Confucius, the most famous Chinese philosopher. Confucius' thought emphasized love and respect for parents and older siblings in the family. It also means respect for authority and older people in general. Even though Kong Rong was an accomplished literary scholar later in life, he was most well known for his good manners toward his brothers as a child. Kong Rong was an extremely bright child. Later he served as a regional governor in Shangdong Province in eastern China. However, as an adult, he did not get along with his superior because of his acerbic personality. Kong Rong purposefully criticized and embarrassed his superior on several occasions. He was executed and died at a young age.

20. The Man and His Horse

The name of the old man in this story is Mr. Sai. "Sai" in Chinese means frontier. This story took place near the northern frontier in China. China borders 14 countries, more than any other country in the world today. Traditionally, Chinese frontiers always presented challenges to the Chinese empire. The northern Chinese frontiers were adjacent to nomadic cultures and tribes since ancient times. The nomadic people, including the Huns, tried to invade China frequently in Chinese history. There were constant wars along the northern Chinese frontiers. The Great Wall of China was begun in the 5th century BCE for defense against nomadic peoples. It was maintained throughout history by different emperors until the 17th century.

The nomadic tribes had taller and faster horses than those from mainland China, so ancient Chinese people desired horses from the nomadic tribes. In this story, when Mr. Sai's lost horse came back with another horse, and his son fell in love with the new horse; it was likely that this new horse was from a nomadic tribe. When young men were drafted for war, it was likely that they were drafted to fight the nomads in the north.

21. The Clam and the Crane

The crane is a symbol of longevity and good luck in Chinese culture. The theme of crane occurs frequently in paintings and arts. The crane is the second most popular bird in Chinese paintings, after the Phoenix. The crane is also associated with Taoism, which is a popular religion in China. Many Taoist monks sought longevity. Cranes often appear among pine trees and bamboos in mountain scenes. "Crane-colored" hair is used as a respectful term to describe an old person in Chinese culture. Old people are much honored in Chinese culture. They are seen as experienced and full of wisdom. An old man is referred to as "Grandpa" by strangers, and an old woman is referred to as "Grandma." Cranes and peaches are two popular designs on birthday cakes or other gift items for old people in China. They symbolize long life and good fortune.

22. The Bamboo Artist

This story is about a famous artist Wen Tong (1018–1079) in the Song Dynasty, which was known for development in arts and literature in Chinese history. The emperors in the Song Dynasty encouraged artists and scholars in their creative work. One of the emperors was a renowned artist, painter, and calligrapher himself.

Common themes in traditional Chinese paintings are birds, flowers, mountains, and people. Bamboo is also a common theme. Bamboo is hollow inside; therefore, it symbolizes humility and honesty. Bamboo is upright and tall, and has incremental growth rings; therefore, it also symbolizes the spirit of growth and improvement. Bamboo is a favorite plant in Chinese gardens. Wen Tong's cousin, Shu Shi, a famous poet and artist in the Song Dynasty, once said, "People can eat meals without meat, but they cannot live without bamboo in the surroundings."

23. Practice

This story illustrates the value of practice making perfection in traditional Chinese thought. Chinese culture emphasizes the value of hard work and the virtue of practice. The word for "skilled, or experienced" is *shou lian*. The character for "Shou" means cooked food; the character for "lian" means boiling raw silk. Hard work in the Chinese mentality is hard labor both mentally and physically, as the pictograph for both words depicts the agony of enduring burning fire. It takes determination and endurance for a person to do hard work. Hard work is the prerequisite to any success. When it applies to study or mastering a skill, hard work means repetition and practice. Chinese children are often required to copy and recite textbooks as a standard homework practice.

24. The Reflection of the Snake

This story tells about a person being sickened at the sight of a reflection of a snake. When people become ill in China, they can go to visit a western-style doctor or a traditional Chinese medicine doctor. Traditional Chinese medicine has a long history of over 3,000 years. Traditional Chinese medicine employs a different method from western medicine. It uses acupuncture and herbs to treat illness.

Traditional Chinese medicine believes the body is made of five basic elements, with each corresponding to the five vital organs. The five elements are wood, fire, earth, metal, and water. Wood is for liver, fire is for heart, earth is for spleen, metal is for lung, and water is for kidney. The five vital organs also have five external corresponding sensory organs. Eyes are related to liver, tongue is related to heart, mouth is related to spleen, nose is related to lung, and ears are related to kidney.

Therefore, according to the theory in traditional Chinese medicine, if a person has hearing problems, it is not only his ears that malfunction, but rather, his kidney may be weak too. In addition to treating the symptoms of the ears, medicine should also be given to treat the hidden problems with the kidney. Traditional Chinese medicine is becoming more and more popular in the West.

25. The Teacher's Mother

Mengzi, also called Mencius, was taught by the grandson of Confucius, a famous Confucian philosopher and teacher in China. Menzi lived during the 4th century BCE. He was considered a Confucian philosopher because he helped spread and establish the Confucian school of thought in China. Like Confucius, Mengzi also traveled to different states to preach his ideas about government and life. An important idea in Mengzi's belief is that human nature is good. Mengzi believed people were born good. However, because there is evil in society and the environment, people learn to be bad. This story reflects this idea. Mengzi's mother was afraid Mengzi would be influenced by an unproductive environment. She chose to relocate several times for Mengzi to be in a good environment that was conducive for study and learning.

Other Books of Interest from Pro Lingua

AESOP'S FABLES. A collection of storytelling cards featuring 48 illustrated stories, many of them known the world over: "The Fox and the Grapes," "The Shepherd Boy and the Wolf." The students choose a card, study it, and then tell stories to each other.

NORTH AMERICAN INDIAN TALES. 48 animal stories collected from tribes across North America. The tales explain how the world came to be as it is. Each story is on a separate card with a colorful illustration by a popular Native American artist.

NASREDDIN HODJA. Stories to read and retell. A collection of short stories known throughout the world of Islam, featuring the great Turkish folk hero Nasreddin Hodja. The readings can be detached from the book and used as prompts for storytelling. A **CD** is available.

PEARLS OF WISDOM. A collection of African and Caribbean folktales for listening and reading. All the tales are dramatically told by Dr. Raouf Mama, a West African griot. Along with the **text** and the CDs, a **student workbook** contains exercises in vocabulary and all skill areas.

HOW AND WHY FOLKTALES FROM AROUND THE WORLD. Twelve stories from a variety of countries, including two from China, for reading and discussing. Each story is accompanied with six pages of language development exercises.

WHERE IN THE WORLD. A beginning level integrated skills text. A traveler goes around the world, visiting, commenting on, and experiencing famous places, including the Great Wall and The Terra Cotta Warriors. **CD**s available.

THE READ AND LEARN SERIES. Four separate, graded readers. In **READ 50**, the average passage is only 50 words long. The other books are **READ 75**, **READ 100**, and **READ 125**. Each reading passage is followed with brief exercises. A wide variety of topics from around the world in various formats. Each book has an accompanying **CD**.

GO FISH. A collection of card games using large cards to be detached from the book. The games focus on the vocabulary of the home. The cards are without words, allowing use in any language. A **Chinese Word List** is available on the web.

LEXICARRY. A vocabulary builder that also stimulates speaking and listening skills. 4500 unlabeled pictures with an English key in the index. Additional WORD LISTS are available in several languages, including **Chinese**.

LIVING IN CHINA. A brief introduction for students, visitors, and business travelers. Includes FIRST STEPS (money, food, driving, health, etc.), CULTURE (manners, gifts, taboos, culture bumps, etc.), FACTS (geography, people, government, etc.), DOING BUSINESS, WORKING, and a short section on LANGUAGE.